**WEST TISBURY FREE PUBLIC LIBRARY**

Presented by

N. Puner

# JASON AND THE BEES

A Nature I CAN READ Book

Harper & Row, Publishers

# JASON
## AND THE
# BEES

STORY AND PICTURES BY

Brom Hoban

FIRST EDITION

Library of Congress Cataloging in Publication Data
Hoban, Abrom.
  Jason and the bees.

  (A Nature I can read book)
  SUMMARY: Jason meets a beekeeper and learns
about bees and their habits.
  1. Bees—Juvenile literature.   2. Bee culture—
Juvenile literature.  [1. Bees]  I. Title.  II. Series:
Nature I can read book.
SF523.5.H6   1980        638'.1        78-13902
ISBN 0-06-022381-2
ISBN 0-06-022382-0 lib. bdg.

*to my mother, a real honey*

Jason was shooting

with his bow and arrows.

He shot the first arrow

way up in the air near a tree.

It fell to the ground.

When Jason went to get it,

he saw a big hole in the tree.

"I saw some bees in that hole,"
said his big sister Elsie.

"That is OK," said Jason.

"I am brave."

"You always cry when
I pull your hair," said Elsie.

"You haven't pulled my hair
in a week," said Jason.

"I am braver now."

Jason shot the arrow again.

It hit the tree near the hole
and fell to the ground.

The bees were buzzing now.

Elsie ran toward the house.

"You are a scaredy-cat," yelled Jason.

"Scaredy-cats don't get stung,"

Elsie said as she slammed the door.

Jason went to get his arrow.

When he picked it up,

there were bees crawling on it.

The bees crawled onto his hand.

There were hundreds of bees.

And none of them stung Jason!

Jason was so surprised

that he was not even scared.

"These bees are my friends,"

said Jason.

He watched them crawl slowly

off his hand.

"I wonder why they do not sting me,"

Jason said.

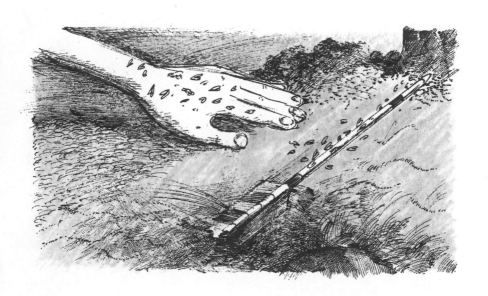

"I wonder why they are so slow."

Jason put his hand down again.

The bees crawled slowly up his arm.

He walked toward the house

with his arm held out.

"Mom! Mom!" yelled Elsie.

"Jason has bees all over him!"

But just then the bees flew off.

The next day Jason went out

to play with his sling-shot.

"Where are you going?" Elsie asked.

"I am going to shoot

some telephone poles," said Jason.

But Jason did not shoot

at telephone poles.

He went around to the back

of the yard where the bees were.

He picked up a stone

and loaded his sling-shot.

"Maybe the bees were too tired
to sting yesterday," he said.
His first shot hit the bees' nest.
The bees started to buzz loudly.
Jason shot them again.

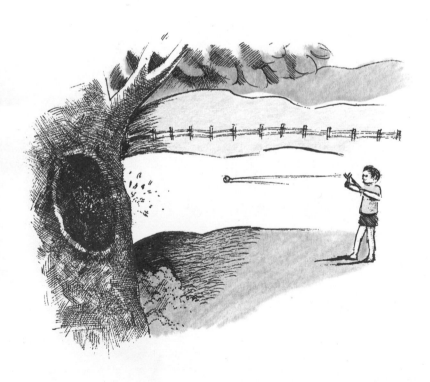

POW! A cloud of bees

buzzed angrily at Jason.

He dropped his sling-shot

and ran.

He ran around and around the house.

"Help! Help!" Jason cried.

Elsie looked out the window

and saw Jason run by.

"Mom! Mom!" Elsie yelled.

"Jason has bees chasing him."

But Jason was already in the house.

"Elsie told me what you did,"

said his mother.

"You have made the bees angry

for no reason."

"I was just trying to find out

about them," said Jason.

"One day they are friendly.

The next day they chase me."

"Well, there must be a better way

to find out about them,"

said his mother.

"You were lucky you were not stung."

Jason went for a ride

on his bicycle to think about bees.

He rode past the bees' nest.

He rode past a fence

and past some pine woods.

He rode past some mailboxes.

Then he saw a little sign.

It read, MR. WEISS, BEEKEEPER.

"I never noticed that before,"

thought Jason.

He climbed over the beekeeper's fence.

There were a lot of white boxes,

and more bees

than Jason had ever seen.

They were flying in every direction.

Jason got a little scared.

He started to run to the fence.

"Hey! Wait a minute.

What's the matter?"

Jason turned and saw a man

in a hat with netting.

In the man's hand was a can

with smoke coming out of it.

"Don't be scared," said the man.

"These are my bees,

and they won't hurt you."

22

"I have never seen so many bees,"
said Jason.

"I don't want them to chase me
or sting me.

I have had trouble with bees."

"You must have been giving

them trouble," said the man.

"By the way, I am Mr. Weiss."

24

"I hit them with some rocks,"
said Jason. "And I'm Jason."
"Well," said Mr. Weiss,
"the bees had a reason to chase you.
They were trying to save their hive."

"But the first time I saw them
they were friendly," said Jason.
"They were all over the tree,
and they crawled on my hand.
None of them stung me!"

"That must have been a *swarm*,"
said Mr. Weiss.
"When a colony or hive gets
too crowded, some of the bees leave.

They fill up with honey
so they will have energy
to start a new hive.

That is why they did not sting you."
"You mean the honey makes
them sweeter?" asked Jason.

"No," said Mr. Weiss.

"The honey makes their stomachs

so full they can't double over.

A bee has to double over to sting.

Look, I'll show you."

Mr. Weiss made some smoke

come out of the can

he was holding.

"What does the smoke do?"

Jason asked.

"When there is smoke, the bees fill up

with honey in case the hive is on fire,"

said Mr. Weiss.

"They get ready to leave

to start a new hive.

See, they can't sting now,"

"Just like when

they were swarming," said Jason.

30

"That is right," said Mr. Weiss.

"I smoke them

so I can look into the hive.

"I look to see how much honey

they are making.

I look to see how many

new eggs there are."

"Can I help?" Jason asked.

"OK," said Mr. Weiss.

"Why don't you stop by tomorrow?"

When he got home, Jason said to Elsie,
"I stood in a swarm of bees,
and none of them stung me."
"I don't believe you," she said.

The next day Jason rode over

to the beekeeper's.

Mr. Weiss was bending over a beehive.

"Here I am!" Jason shouted.

Mr. Weiss jumped.

"Never startle a beekeeper,"

he warned.

"You have to be careful

when you are working with bees.

They don't like loud noises

or sudden movements."

Jason walked carefully
over to the hive and looked in.
"Why are some of the bees
smaller?" asked Jason.

"They are females, the worker bees.
They do all the work," said Mr. Weiss.
"They build the hive
and gather the *nectar*.
The honey bee lands on the flower
to suck the nectar.
Nectar looks like tiny drops
inside a flower.

"The flower has *pollen* in it, too.

The pollen sticks to the bees'

hairy legs.

The bees bring the nectar and

pollen back to the hive

and make honey.

WORKERS

A worker bee works so hard

in the summer that she will live only

for about six weeks.

Old, tired bees are carried

far away by the others

and left to die."

"Boy," said Jason. "That

does not seem fair."

DRONE

"Well," said Mr. Weiss, "see the bees

with the big eyes?

They are males, the drones.

They are not treated much better.

Their only job is to mate

with the queen bee.

She mates only one time.

After a drone mates with the queen,

he dies.

And the rest of the drones

are not fed by the workers.

But the queen

keeps on laying drone eggs

so there will always be new drones.

If a queen dies or becomes too old,

new drones will be needed to mate

with the new queen."

"I am glad I am not a drone!"

said Jason.

"But if I were, I don't think

I would mate with the queen."

QUEEN

"You would try to," said Mr. Weiss.
"With their large eyes, the drones
can see the queen fly out
on her wedding flight.
She flies very high, so only the drone
that flies the highest
can mate with her."

"Bees do a lot more than I thought,"
said Jason.
"I won't hit them with rocks anymore."

The next time Jason

went to the beekeeper's,

Mr. Weiss had something for him.

It was a beekeeper's hat.

It was just like Mr. Weiss's,

except it was smaller.

44

"Now I can look into the hives like you do," said Jason. "What are you looking for this time?"

"To see if the queen is laying enough worker eggs and not too many drone eggs," said Mr. Weiss. "Drone eggs are bigger.

If there are lots of small eggs

I know she is doing a good job.

A queen can lay 1,000 eggs a day.

And it takes 21 days for an egg

to become a baby bee."

"I guess that is why the queen

is so big," said Jason.

"She has to lay a lot of eggs."

"That is right," said Mr. Weiss.

"It takes 20,000 bees to collect

a pound of nectar.

And a pound of nectar makes only

a quarter of a pound of honey."

Mr. Weiss reached into the hive

and picked up a piece of honeycomb.

He pointed to the dark color

in the comb.

"This shows the bees are making

plenty of honey," he said.

"The bees eat the honey
and grow strong."
"How much honey do you get to take?"
asked Jason.
"I take everything over
sixty pounds in a hive,"
said Mr. Weiss.

"The fall is the best time
for me to take the honey,"
Mr. Weiss added.
"That is when most flowers
have bloomed.
Sometimes I get
as much as 100 pounds
from a single hive!

If it is a good season for flowers,
it is a good season for honey."

The next day Elsie saw Jason

with his beekeeper's hat.

"What is that?" she asked.

"It is a beekeeper's hat,"

said Jason proudly.

"I am going to the beekeeper's."

"I am coming with you," said Elsie.

"No, you are not," said Jason.

"You would be scared of all the bees.

You have to be brave

to be a beekeeper."

"If you can do it, I can too,"

said Elsie.

"Besides, I am older than you,

and I can pull your hair."

"No you can't," shouted Jason.

Jason put on his beekeeper's hat

and rode over to see Mr. Weiss.

He waited for Mr. Weiss

to come down to the hives.

Suddenly he saw Elsie

walking among the beehives.

"Go home," Jason shouted.

"You are not allowed!"

"I just want to see

what you do with the bees,"

said Elsie.

"If you don't go, I'll make the bees
go after you," said Jason.
Elsie grabbed his beekeeper's hat
and ran.
Jason chased after her.

They ran around and around the hives.

Then Jason tripped

and knocked over a beehive.

Angry bees flew out of the fallen hive.

Elsie put on the beekeeper's hat

and was not stung.

But one bee found Jason,

and he got a sting

on the tip of his nose.

58

"Ow! Ow!" yelled Jason.
"Why can't you be stung?
Why can't I be friends
with the bees?"
"Well, why can't you
be friends with me?"
asked Elsie.

Mr. Weiss came out.

He did not say anything.

He picked up the beehive,

and saw that it was all right.

Then he said, "Maybe now
you will be more careful
near your hive."

"*My* hive?" asked Jason.

"Yes," said Mr. Weiss, "your hive.
See, look over here."

Jason looked and saw his name
was on a hive.

He stood up and took his
beekeeper's hat back.

"It will be a while

before you are old enough

to take care of the hive yourself,"

said Mr. Weiss.

"But I will help you until then."

"Thanks!" said Jason. "Thanks a lot!"

"What about me?" asked Elsie.

"Well," said Jason, "I'll give you

some of my honey

if you promise not to pull

my hair anymore."

"OK," said Elsie.

Jason and Elsie rode home
on their bicycles together.
And Jason hardly felt
the bee sting on his nose.

Jason and the bees
Brom Hoban

# DATE DUE

| | | | |
|---|---|---|---|
| SEP 16 2015 | | | |
| | | | |
| | | | |
| | | | |
| | | | |
| | | | |
| | | | |
| | | | |
| | | | |
| | | | |

PRINTED IN U.S.A.